Nature
Detectives

First published in 2008
by Wayland

This paperback edition published in 2009

Wayland
338 Euston Road
London NW1 3BH

Wayland Australia
Level 17/207 Kent Street
Sydney, NSW 2000

Series Editor: Louise John
Editor: Katie Powell
Cover design: Paul Cherrill
Design: D.R.ink
Consultant: Shirley Bickler

A CIP catalogue record for this book is available from the British Library.

ISBN 9780750255288 (hbk)
ISBN 9780750255295 (pbk)

Printed in China

Wayland is a division of Hachette Children's Books

Nature
Detectives

Written by Pippa Goodhart
Illustrated by Sue Mason

WAYLAND

The class went to find wild animals in the woods.

"I can see Nasim," said Jake.
"He's quite wild."

"Grrrr!" said Nasim.

"Don't be silly," said
Miss Samson.

"Let's see how many animals live in the woods," said Miss Samson. "How can we tell if an animal has been here?"

"It leaves clues," said Bella.

"I've found a black feather," said Nasim.

"That's a good clue," said Miss Samson.

"A blackbird must have dropped it," said Bella.

"This is like being a detective!" said Nasim. "Go and find a clue then," said Jake.

"There!" said Nasim and he pointed. "A horse's hoof prints."

"Look at this!" said Bella.
"Here's another clue. A hole.
Maybe a rabbit lives here."

"And look at these prints!"
said Jake. "A funny
animal with lots of paws!"

"This animal has a tail, too," said Jake. "Here's a big, fat tail mark. Look!"

"It must be enormous!"
said Bella.

"What sort of animal is it?"
said Jake.
"I don't know," said Bella.

"Let's go back to Miss Samson," said Jake.

"No!" said Nasim. "Let's follow the paw prints and find the animal!"

"Shush!" said Jake.
"It might hear us!"

"Do you think it eats children?" asked Bella. "Maybe," said Nasim.

"It's coming this way!" said Jake. "What if it's a monster?"

"Perhaps it's following US!" said Nasim.

"What was that noise?"
said Jake. "Stop!"

But Bella and Nasim
went on.

Then Jake started to laugh.
"What's funny?" said Bella.

"Look!" said Jake. "The monster is us. Our wellies are making the footprints...

...and Nasim's bag made the tail print! We've just walked round in a circle."

Mrs Samson laughed, too.
"Come on, everyone.
It's picnic time," she said.

"Come and have some sandwiches, you monsters!"

START READING is a series of highly enjoyable books for beginner readers. **The books have been carefully graded to match the Book Bands widely used in schools.** This enables readers to be sure they choose books that match their own reading ability.

Look out for the Band colour on the book in our Start Reading logo.

The Bands are:

Pink Band 1

Red Band 2

Yellow Band 3

Blue Band 4

Green Band 5

Orange Band 6

Turquoise Band 7

Purple Band 8

Gold Band 9

START READING books can be read independently or shared with an adult. They promote the enjoyment of reading through satisfying stories supported by fun illustrations.

Pippa Goodhart lives with her husband, three daughters, a dog, a cat and four chickens who all leave interesting footprints on her floors. She found learning to read hard, but now loves reading, and writing, books.

Sue Mason grew up in East Sussex, surrounded by trees, eating crumpets. She illustrates from a happy little studio called The Chocolate Factory, which she shares with special friends. Sometimes they break from work to have a little dance around and eat cake.